This book is dedicated to Claudia and Kate
(and long-suffering Moms everywhere) –L.P.

tiger tales
an imprint of ME Media, LLC
202 Old Ridgefield Road, Wilton, CT 06897
Published in the United States 2008
Originally published in Great Britain 2008
by Little Tiger Press
an imprint of Magi Publications
Text and illustrations copyright © 2008 Liz Pichon
CIP data is available
ISBN-13: 978-1-58925-077-2
ISBN-10: 1-58925-077-X
Printed in Singapore

The Three Horrid Little Pigs

by Liz Pichon

tiger tales

Once upon a time, three horrid
little pigs lived with their mother
in a tiny house.

The little pigs were very bad
and they drove their mother crazy!

"I've had enough of you pesky pigs," she told them. "It's about time you moved out and made your own way in the world!"

So she packed their bags and sent them away.

OUT!

Stop pushing!

The first horrid little pig came across a big pile of straw. "This straw is PERFECT for me to build my house," he thought.

But the little pig was lazy, and he didn't make his straw house very strong at all.

Luckily, a big friendly wolf (who just happened to be a builder) was passing by.

"Good grief!" said the wolf. "What a mess that house is. I'll see if I can help."

Gasp!

Good enough.

"Little pig, little pig, may I come in?" asked the wolf. "NO WAY!" shouted the pig. "Not by the hairs of my chinny chin chin will I let a WOLF in!

Put one paw on my house

Oh dear!

and I'll **huff** and I'll **puff** and I'll

KICK YOU OUT!"

"I only wanted to help," said the wolf sadly,
as he went on his way.

The second horrid little pig found a huge pile of twigs. "These twigs will make a great house for me!" he thought. But the little pig was even **lazier** than his brother...

so the house was a disaster!

When the friendly wolf saw the terrible tangle of twigs, he thought, "Oh no! That house is an accident waiting to happen. I'd better help."

Goodness me!

"Little pig, little pig, may I come in?" asked the wolf.

"GET LOST!" shouted the rude little pig. "Not by the hairs of my chinny chin chin will I let a WOLF in!

Put one paw on my house and I'll huff

MOVE IT, WOLFY!

and I'll **puff**

and I'll

THROW

YOU

RIGHT

OUT!"

"I'm sorry," said the wolf.
"I only wanted to help."

How rude!

The third horrid little pig was SO lazy, he couldn't be bothered to build a house at all. So he found a nice chicken coop instead ... and moved in.

The friendly wolf just happened to be nearby.

"Oh my!" he thought. "Those poor chickens! I must speak to that pig."

Pig stole our house!

HELP!

"Little pig, little pig, may I come in?"

"SCRAM!" shouted the pig. "Not by the hairs of my chinny chin chin will I let a WOLF in! Put one paw on my house and I'll **huff** ...

and I'll **puff** and I'll ..."

"Hold it right there!" said the wolf. "This isn't YOUR house. It's the chickens' house."

"Who cares?" said the little pig. "Now go away—ALL OF YOU!"

What a horrid little pig he was.

Charming!

So the kind wolf invited all the chickens back to HIS house, which was built from bricks and very strong indeed.

WOLF'S HOUSE

Meanwhile, the house built by the first horrid little pig ...

COWS'
STRAW

was being eaten up by a
herd of hungry cows.

The house built by the
second horrid little pig . . .

was being pulled apart
by a flock of angry birds.

And the third horrid little pig . . .

*You've taken
our TWIGS!*

Our NESTS!

was being pecked by
a rooster and went WEE WEE WEEEEEEEE EEEEEEEE all the way back to
his brothers.

(Which was *just* what
the rooster wanted.)

Now NONE of the pigs had a home. But the wolf did. And it looked warm and cozy.

"This house would be perfect for us," said the horrid little pigs.

So they waited until dark.
Then they climbed onto the roof
and began to slide down the chimney.
The wolf heard the horrid little pigs, so he got out a
GREAT BIG POT OF BOILING...

SOUP!

"You must be hungry," said the wolf.

He really was the sweetest, loveliest wolf ever.

The friendly wolf let the pigs stay. And after a while they stopped being lazy, horrid little pigs and learned how to build a sturdy house made of bricks...

which was big enough
for EVERYONE!

And they all lived
happily ever after.

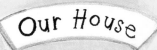

The End